Haunting Highways: Real-Life Ghost Stories from Truck Drivers

Joseph Capps

Published by Joseph Capps, 2024.

HAUNTING HIGHWAYS: REAL-LIFE GHOST STORIES FROM TRUCK DRIVERS

First edition. September 19, 2024.

ISBN: 979-8224386468

Written by Joseph Capps.

Also by Joseph Capps

ChatGPT for Beginners: A Comprehensive Guide
Whispers from Beyond: An Exploration of Ghosts and the Paranormal"
Haunting Highways: Real-Life Ghost Stories from Truck Drivers
The Road Ahead: A Comprehensive Guide to Trucking in the United
States

Table of Contents

Title: Haunting Highways: Real-Life Ghost Stories from Truck Drivers

Table of Contents

Introduction

The life of a truck driver is often depicted as a solitary journey through endless highways, dotted with truck stops and rest areas. However, between the miles driven and the stories shared, there's a rich tapestry of experiences that often includes encounters with the supernatural. This e-book aims to capture the essence of those encounters—stories that blur the lines between reality and the unknown.

Throughout the chapters, you'll find firsthand accounts from truck drivers who have faced inexplicable events during their travels. Whether it's a phantom hitchhiker appearing on a desolate stretch of road or the unsettling feeling of being watched at a quiet rest stop, these stories serve as a reminder that the open road holds more than just miles—it holds memories, legends, and perhaps, a few lingering spirits.

—-

Chapter 1: The Phantom Hitchhiker

The open road is a peculiar place, often filled with the hum of tires on asphalt, the rhythm of a steady engine, and the solitude that comes with long hours behind the wheel. For truck drivers, it's a world of routine and familiarity, yet it's also a realm where the unexpected lurks just around the corner. One of the most chilling experiences that many drivers share is their encounter with the phantom hitchhiker—a spectral figure that appears on the side of the road, leaving a haunting impression long after the moment has passed.

A Tale from Interstate 95

Mike Thompson had been driving trucks for over a decade. The scent of burnt diesel and the sound of his favorite country music playlist were his constant companions. He knew the ins and outs of the highways across the eastern United States like the back of his hand. On one particular night, while cruising along Interstate 95, the world outside his cab faded into a blur of darkness. The vast emptiness of the road stretched out before him, illuminated only by the beams of his headlights, which carved through the night like a knife through fog.

As he navigated a deserted stretch of highway, his mind began to wander, the exhaustion of the long haul creeping in. Suddenly, something caught his eye. There, under the flickering light of a distant streetlamp, stood a figure. Dressed in a long, vintage coat that billowed slightly in the night breeze, the figure raised a thumb, a stark contrast against the shadows. Mike's heart raced; he wasn't one to stop for hitchhikers, but something compelled him to pull over.

The Encounter

As the truck came to a halt, Mike's mind raced with questions. Who was this person? What were they doing out here alone? He opened the passenger door, and the figure climbed in with a grace that seemed almost otherworldly.

"Thank you for stopping," the hitchhiker said, their voice low and melodic, carrying an unusual calm that soothed Mike's nerves. As he glanced over, he was struck by the hitchhiker's eyes—deep and dark, yet sparkling with a strange light that seemed to reflect the stars above.

"Where are you headed?" he asked, trying to make conversation and dispel the odd tension hanging in the air.

"Just ahead, a few miles down," they replied cryptically, their gaze fixated on the road ahead as if they could see into the future.

The two engaged in light conversation about the road, the weather, and life on the highway. The hitchhiker spoke with an eloquence that fascinated Mike, sharing stories that blended nostalgia with a haunting beauty. They spoke of dreams and lost loves, weaving tales that felt both real and surreal, like snippets from a long-forgotten movie. Time seemed to stretch and contract in the cab, as if the very fabric of reality was bending around them.

Mike felt a connection he couldn't explain, as if he had known this person in another life. The air in the cab grew heavier, charged with an unspoken understanding. Yet, beneath that connection, a sense of unease lurked, whispering that something was not quite right.

The Sudden Vanishing

Just as they approached a quiet exit, Mike glanced over to point out a landmark he had passed countless times. But when he turned back to his passenger, he was met with an empty seat. The hitchhiker had vanished without a trace.

Confused and shaken, Mike slammed on the brakes, his heart racing. He looked around frantically, searching for any sign of the mysterious figure, but the road was empty. The only sound was the hum of the engine and the rustle of the wind outside, which had suddenly grown cold and foreboding.

After a few moments of disbelief, Mike continued driving, his mind racing with questions. Had he imagined the entire encounter? Or had he truly picked up a hitchhiker who wasn't of this world? The feeling of loss settled over him like a heavy blanket, and he couldn't shake the sense that something profound had just occurred.

Theories Behind the Legend

As Mike shared his story with fellow truckers at rest stops, he learned he was not alone in his experience. Tales of the phantom hitchhiker have circulated among drivers for decades, particularly along lonely stretches of road. Many believe that these spectral figures are souls seeking closure, or those who met untimely ends in tragic accidents.

Some speculate that the hitchhikers are guardians, appearing to warn drivers of impending danger or to guide them safely through the night. Others see them as reminders of the fragility of life, encouraging drivers to appreciate the moments they have on the road.

Mike's encounter left him with more questions than answers. It became a defining moment in his life as a truck driver, a story that would be retold many times over the years. The phantom hitchhiker had become part of his journey, a testament to the mysteries that linger just beyond the headlights—a reminder that the road is not just a passage but a place where the living and the lost intertwine.

In the days that followed, Mike often found himself glancing in the passenger seat, half-expecting to see the hitchhiker there, sharing stories of the road. Though the memory of that night would fade with time, the lesson it imparted would remain etched in his mind: that sometimes, the open road is more than just a path to a destination; it is a bridge to the unknown, where every mile tells a story waiting to be discovered.

Chapter 2: The Haunted Rest Stop

The life of a truck driver is often filled with long hours on the road, endless stretches of highway, and the occasional stop at a rest area. For many, these stops are necessary breaks to recharge, grab a bite to eat, or simply stretch their legs. However, some rest areas come with a reputation that sends chills down the spine of even the most seasoned drivers. One such place is a rest stop in Nebraska, notorious among truckers for its unsettling atmosphere and eerie occurrences.

A Night in Nebraska

It was a cool autumn evening when Sarah Jenkins, a long-haul truck driver, found herself on a remote stretch of highway in Nebraska. The sun dipped below the horizon, casting long shadows across the road, and the chill of the impending night settled in. After hours of driving, she decided it was time to take a break. The flickering lights of a rest stop appeared in the distance, and she pulled in, grateful for the chance to stretch her legs.

As Sarah stepped out of her truck, the crisp air filled her lungs, refreshing yet foreboding. The rest area was eerily quiet, with only the sound of leaves rustling in the wind. She walked toward the restroom, her footsteps echoing against the pavement. The fluorescent lights buzzed overhead, casting a harsh glow that only heightened her sense of unease.

Strange Noises and Eerie Shadows

As Sarah finished her business and headed back outside, she felt a shiver run down her spine. The night had grown darker, and the shadows seemed to dance around her. She glanced toward the picnic area, where a few wooden tables sat under the faint light. That's when she heard it—a low, mournful sound that seemed to rise from the ground itself.

Curiosity piqued, she approached the source of the noise, her heart racing. The sound was reminiscent of someone weeping, the sobs echoing through the stillness of the night. As she got closer, she noticed a figure seated at one of the tables, head bowed and shoulders shaking as if in sorrow.

"Hey, are you okay?" Sarah called out, her voice trembling slightly.

The figure lifted their head, revealing a pale face with deep-set eyes that glimmered with unshed tears. "I'm fine," they replied, their voice haunting yet soft. "Just lost in thought."

Sarah felt an unsettling chill as she took a step back. The figure wore old-fashioned clothing, and their demeanor seemed out of place in the modern rest area. A sense of familiarity washed over her, as if she had entered a scene from another time.

Historical Background of the Location

Intrigued yet unnerved, Sarah did some research in the days that followed. She learned that the rest stop had a dark history. Years ago, it was the site of a tragic accident involving a family traveling through Nebraska. Their vehicle had skidded off the road during a storm, claiming the lives of the parents, while their young daughter had vanished without a trace. The rest area had since become a site of ghostly encounters, with drivers reporting sightings of a little girl playing near the picnic tables and the sound of soft cries echoing through the night.

The more Sarah learned, the more she felt a connection to the place. The figure she had encountered was likely the spirit of the girl, lost in a loop of sorrow, yearning for her family. The notion was both heart-wrenching and frightening, leaving Sarah with a sense of urgency to honor the memory of the lost souls.

An Unexpected Encounter

Determined to confront her fears, Sarah returned to the rest stop a week later, armed with a small bouquet of flowers. As she approached the picnic area, she felt a strange energy surrounding her, almost as if the air were charged with emotion. She placed the flowers on the table where she had seen the figure and whispered a few words of comfort.

"Your story matters. You're not forgotten."

As she turned to leave, she felt a gentle breeze caress her cheek, accompanied by the faint sound of laughter. Startled, Sarah looked back, and for a brief moment, she saw the figure of the little girl standing at the edge of the picnic area, smiling softly. The girl's eyes sparkled with gratitude, and then she vanished into thin air, leaving Sarah with a sense of peace and closure.

Reflections on the Experience

In the days that followed, Sarah shared her encounter with fellow truck drivers. Many had similar stories about the haunted rest stop, each tale adding another layer to the legend. They spoke of strange occurrences—flickering lights, ghostly whispers, and the feeling of being watched.

The experience at the Nebraska rest stop became a pivotal moment for Sarah. It taught her that the road is not just a physical journey but an emotional one, filled with stories of those who came before. The ghosts of the past linger on the highways, reminding us of the fragility of life and the connections we share with one another, even across the boundaries of time and space.

As she continued her travels, Sarah carried the memory of the little girl with her, a reminder that every mile traveled holds the potential for encounters with the unknown. The open road, she realized, is a tapestry of lives interwoven with stories, some heartwarming, others heart-wrenching, but all deserving of remembrance.

Rest stops, often seen as mere pit stops for weary travelers, have become the backdrop for numerous myths and urban legends, particularly in the realm of the supernatural. Here are some common myths and urban legends associated with rest areas:

1. **The Vanishing Hitchhiker**: This classic urban legend involves a driver picking up a hitchhiker, only to discover that the passenger disappears from the vehicle, often leaving behind a personal item like a

scarf or a coat. Variations of this legend often feature the hitchhiker as a ghost seeking closure or revenge.

2. **The Woman in White**: Many rest stops are said to be haunted by the spirit of a woman in white, often depicted as a lost soul searching for her family. She is typically described as appearing at night, wandering the area, and sometimes trying to flag down passing cars.

3. **Ghostly Laughter or Crying Children**: Drivers have reported hearing laughter or the sounds of children playing in or around rest stops, especially late at night. These sounds are often attributed to the spirits of children who died tragically near the location.

4. **The Creepy Restroom**: Urban legends often mention restrooms at certain rest stops being haunted or cursed. Stories abound of strange noises, flickering lights, or even sightings of ghostly figures appearing in mirrors or through the cracks of stalls.

5. **The Phantom Truck Driver**: Some rest stops have stories of a ghostly truck driver who appears to warn other drivers of danger on the road or to help those in distress. This figure is often said to vanish once the warning is given.

6. **The Haunted Picnic Area**: Many rest areas have picnic tables that are rumored to be haunted. Legends suggest that travelers have experienced sudden chills, feelings of being watched, or even sightings of ghostly figures while resting at these tables.

7. **Animal Spirits**: In rural areas, rest stops may be associated with legends of animal spirits, such as deer or dogs, that appear to guide travelers or serve as omens of danger. These spirits are often seen as protectors of the road.

8. **Mysterious Disappearances**: Some urban legends involve travelers who have mysteriously disappeared after stopping at a particular rest area. These stories often suggest that the area is cursed or that a sinister force is at work.

9. **The Phantom Vehicle**: There are tales of a ghostly vehicle that appears on the road near a rest stop, often forewarning drivers of an

accident or danger ahead. The vehicle may vanish when approached, leaving drivers confused and shaken.

10. **The Cursed Location**: Certain rest stops are said to be built on ancient burial grounds or sites of tragic events, leading to legends of curses or hauntings associated with those who stop there.

These myths and urban legends add an intriguing layer to the experience of stopping at a rest area, turning a mundane break into a potential encounter with the supernatural. Whether rooted in truth or simply the product of collective imagination, these stories continue to captivate and terrify travelers.

Chapter 3: The Ghostly Truck

The life of a long-haul truck driver is often characterized by solitude and the rhythmic hum of the open road. As the miles stretch on, the landscape changes, and a myriad of stories unfolds. Among these tales, one of the most chilling is that of the ghostly truck—an apparition that appears on lonely highways, evoking both fear and fascination in those who encounter it.

A Journey Through the Appalachian Mountains

It was a crisp autumn evening when Jake Miller, a seasoned truck driver, set out on a long haul through the winding roads of the Appalachian Mountains. The sun dipped low in the sky, casting a golden hue over the trees, and as twilight settled in, Jake felt a familiar thrill at the thought of the journey ahead. The mountains held their own magic, and he had always found solace in their embrace.

As the night deepened, the temperature dropped, and the shadows lengthened. Jake's thoughts drifted as he navigated the serpentine roads, his truck rumbling steadily beneath him. Suddenly, he caught sight of headlights in his rearview mirror. A truck was tailing him closely, its lights shining brightly against the darkness.

Witnessing a Mysterious Vehicle

At first, Jake thought nothing of it. After all, truckers often travel in packs, sharing the road for safety and camaraderie. But as the minutes ticked by, he noticed that the truck behind him was behaving oddly. It seemed to weave in and out of his lane, never quite gaining ground or falling too far behind. Jake's unease grew as he glanced at the dashboard clock—where had the time gone?

He decided to pull over at a rest area, hoping the other truck would continue on its way. As he parked, he watched the headlights of the mysterious vehicle flash past him, but when he turned to look, the truck was nowhere to be seen. Just a moment ago, it had been right behind him, and now it had vanished into thin air.

Feeling a chill creep up his spine, Jake stepped out of his truck. The air was still and cold, and an unsettling silence enveloped the rest area. He glanced around, half-expecting to see another driver, but the place was deserted. It was then that he noticed something peculiar—a faint glow in the distance, just beyond the tree line.

Local Folklore and Ghost Towns

Driven by curiosity, Jake ventured toward the light. As he approached, he realized it was emanating from an old, rusted truck parked under a gnarled tree. The vehicle appeared to be from a different era, its paint chipped and faded, yet it shimmered with an ethereal quality that set it apart from the surroundings.

Suddenly, he felt an overwhelming sense of dread wash over him. The air grew thick, and the temperature dropped even further. He could see the outline of a figure behind the wheel, illuminated by the glow. Jake's heart raced as he took a cautious step closer.

The figure turned to face him, and Jake was met with the hollow gaze of a long-dead truck driver. The ghostly apparition wore a faded cap and a weary expression, as if burdened by the weight of countless miles traveled. Jake's breath caught in his throat; he was face-to-face with the spirit of a trucker who had likely met a tragic end on these very roads.

The Haunting Story

As the ghostly truck driver raised a hand, Jake felt an inexplicable pull, as if the spirit was trying to communicate. In that moment, he understood the legend that had circulated among truckers for years—that of the ghostly truck that roamed the Appalachian Mountains, seeking solace or perhaps vengeance, eternally bound to the road.

Jake quickly retreated, fear propelling him back to his own truck. Climbing into the cab, he slammed the door shut and locked it, his heart racing. He glanced back at the old truck, but it had vanished, the glow extinguished as if it had never been there.

For the rest of the journey, Jake couldn't shake the feeling of being watched. He drove with heightened caution, each bend in the road reminding him of the ghostly encounter. When he finally reached his destination, he shared his story with fellow drivers, who nodded knowingly. They spoke of the legend of the ghostly truck that roamed the mountains, a warning to those who dared to travel alone at night.

Reflections on the Encounter

Jake's experience left a lasting impression on him. He realized that the road is not merely a path to a destination; it is a living entity, rich with history and echoing with the stories of those who have traveled it before. The ghostly truck driver was a reminder of the dangers and sacrifices that come with the life of a long-haul trucker.

As he continued his journeys, Jake carried the memory of that night with him. The Appalachian Mountains held many secrets, and he understood that he was part of a larger tapestry of stories woven together by the miles driven and the souls encountered along the way.

The open road became not just a means of travel, but a connection to the past—a reminder that those who have come before are never truly gone, as long as their stories are shared and remembered.

—-

Ghost stories associated with highways and roads are prevalent in many cultures around the world. These tales often reflect local beliefs, historical events, and the fears of travelers. Here are some common ghost stories from various cultures:

1. **La Llorona (Mexico)**: This legendary figure, known as "The Weeping Woman," is said to haunt rivers and roads, crying for her lost children. According to the tale, she drowned her children in a fit of rage and now wanders, eternally searching for them. Many believe that hearing her cries near water or while driving at night can lead to misfortune.

2. **The Ghost of the Woman in White (Various Cultures)**: Many cultures have variations of the "Woman in White" ghost who appears on highways or rural roads. Often, she is depicted as a lost soul seeking help, typically having died tragically. In some versions, she lures drivers to help her, only to vanish or cause accidents.

3. **The Phantom Hitchhiker (United States and Beyond)**: This urban legend features a hitchhiker who mysteriously disappears from a driver's vehicle. Often, the hitchhiker is revealed to be a ghost seeking closure or to warn the living of danger. Variations exist in many cultures, highlighting the universal themes of loss and the unknown.

4. **The Headless Horseman (United States)**: Originating from Washington Irving's "The Legend of Sleepy Hollow," this story tells of a ghostly soldier who lost his head during battle and now roams the roads, particularly at night. He is often depicted as chasing after travelers, especially near bridges or dark wooded areas.

5. **The Grey Man (Scotland)**: This ghost is said to haunt the A75 highway in southwestern Scotland. Legend has it that he appears to warn drivers of impending danger, particularly during storms. Some believe that seeing him can prevent car accidents or other misfortunes.

6. **The Ghost of the Taman Shud Case (Australia)**: This mysterious case involves an unidentified man found dead on Somerton Beach in 1948, with a cryptic note in his pocket. Over the years, ghost stories have developed around the area, with sightings of a figure resembling the man near the highway close to the beach.

7. **The Lady in Red (Various Cultures)**: Similar to the Woman in White, the Lady in Red is often depicted as a spirit wearing a red dress, who appears on highways and rural roads. She is sometimes associated with tragic love stories or accidents, and drivers who encounter her may experience a sense of dread or impending doom.

8. **Dandara (Brazil)**: In Brazilian folklore, Dandara is a spirit that roams the highways, particularly in rural areas. Some say she appears to

travelers in need, offering guidance, while others warn that encountering her can lead to bad luck.

9. **The Phantom Driver (Japan)**: In Japanese urban legends, there are stories of ghostly drivers who appear out of nowhere to offer rides or chase down other drivers. These encounters often leave the living feeling unsettled, as the phantom driver typically vanishes without a trace.

10. **The Black-Eyed Children (United States)**: This modern urban legend involves children with black eyes who appear at night, often near highways, asking for help or a ride. Those who encounter them report an overwhelming sense of fear and the feeling that something is very wrong.

These ghost stories reflect cultural beliefs about death, loss, and the supernatural, often serving as cautionary tales for travelers. They highlight the universal fears associated with the unknown and the many ways in which cultures interpret the presence of spirits in the world around them.

Chapter 4: The Lost Love

The road is a tapestry woven with the stories of countless travelers, each journey marked by moments of joy, sorrow, and everything in between. For some, the open highway becomes a place of reflection, a sanctuary for memories that linger long after the miles have been traveled. In this chapter, we explore the poignant tale of lost love that unfolds on the winding roads of Route 66, a historic highway steeped in nostalgia and heartache.

A Journey Down Route 66

Emily Carter was a young woman with a restless spirit, yearning for adventure and the thrill of the open road. Having just graduated from college, she decided to embark on a solo road trip along Route 66, a journey that had long been on her bucket list. With her trusty old pickup truck packed with essentials, she set out, eager to explore the iconic highway.

As she drove through the picturesque landscapes of the American Southwest, Emily felt a sense of freedom wash over her. The sun-drenched deserts, charming roadside diners, and quirky attractions all contributed to the feeling that she was living out her dreams. However, beneath her excitement lingered a bittersweet ache—a recent breakup that left her heart heavy with memories of love lost.

The Unexpected Stop

One evening, as the sun dipped below the horizon, painting the sky in hues of orange and pink, Emily pulled into a small, unassuming rest stop. It was a quiet stretch of road, flanked by tall cacti and the distant hum of crickets. She parked her truck and decided to take a moment to reflect, sitting on a bench overlooking the vast desert landscape.

As she gazed into the distance, her thoughts drifted back to Alex, her college sweetheart. They had shared dreams of traveling the country together, exploring new places, and building a life filled with adventure.

But life had other plans, and their relationship ended abruptly, leaving Emily heartbroken and searching for closure.

A Mysterious Encounter

Lost in her thoughts, Emily was startled by the sound of footsteps approaching. She turned to see a man in his late twenties, dressed in casual clothes, with a warm smile that instantly put her at ease. He introduced himself as Jake, an avid traveler who had been on the road for weeks.

They struck up a conversation, sharing stories of their journeys and the places they had visited. As they talked, Emily felt a connection with Jake—a sense of understanding that resonated deep within her. He spoke of love lost and the importance of cherishing memories while forging ahead.

"You know," Jake said, his voice softening, "sometimes, the road has a way of bringing us back to the people we've loved, even if they're no longer in our lives. It's as if the journey itself helps us find closure."

Emily nodded, feeling a sense of comfort in his words. The conversation flowed effortlessly, and for the first time in weeks, she allowed herself to laugh and enjoy the moment.

A Haunting Revelation

As the sun began to set, casting long shadows across the desert, Emily and Jake took a walk along a nearby trail. The air was filled with the scent of sagebrush, and the tranquility of the moment wrapped around them like a warm embrace. It was then that Jake paused, his expression turning serious.

"There's something I need to share with you," he said, his voice barely above a whisper. "This rest stop is known for its ghost stories. People say that if you sit quietly and listen, you might hear the whispers of lost loves."

Intrigued, Emily leaned in closer. "What do you mean?"

"There's a legend about a couple who used to come here every year. They were deeply in love, but a tragic accident took the man's life. Now, his spirit is said to roam the area, searching for his beloved. Sometimes, people who come here feel his presence and hear him calling out for her."

Emily felt a chill run down her spine, but it was mixed with an inexplicable sense of connection. She closed her eyes, allowing the stillness of the night to envelop her. As she listened intently, she could almost hear a faint whisper carried by the wind, echoing through the desert.

A Moment of Closure

In that moment, Emily understood that her journey was not just about exploring new places; it was also about finding closure for the love she had lost. The memories of Alex flooded back, but instead of pain, she felt a sense of gratitude for the time they shared.

As the stars began to twinkle overhead, Emily opened her eyes, and to her surprise, Jake had vanished. She looked around, bewildered, but there was no sign of him—just the vast desert stretching out before her.

Realizing that Jake might have been a manifestation of her own longing for connection, she felt a profound sense of peace wash over her. The whispers of love lost had guided her to a moment of understanding, allowing her to let go of the heartache that had weighed her down.

Reflections on Love and Loss

With renewed purpose, Emily returned to her truck, ready to continue her journey down Route 66. The road stretched out before her, a reminder that life is a series of twists and turns, filled with moments of joy and sorrow. She carried the memory of Jake and the lost couple with her, understanding that love transcends time and space.

As she drove into the night, the open highway ahead felt like a canvas, waiting for new memories to be painted upon it. The echoes of lost love mingled with the thrill of adventure, reminding her that while some people may fade from our lives, their stories remain etched in our hearts.

The journey continued, and with each mile, Emily felt lighter, ready to embrace the future with open arms, knowing that the road would always lead her to new beginnings.

—-

Numerous highways across the United States are steeped in ghost stories and urban legends, often tied to tragic events, historical significance, or local folklore. Here are some popular ghost stories associated with famous highways:

1. **Route 66 - The Ghost of the Hitchhiker**: Along the iconic Route 66, many travelers have reported encounters with a ghostly hitchhiker. The story often involves a driver picking up a young woman who later disappears from the vehicle, leaving behind an item like a scarf or purse. Some versions suggest that she was killed in a tragic accident while trying to get home.

2. **Interstate 70 - The Phantom Truck**: On stretches of Interstate 70, particularly in the Midwest, drivers have reported sightings of a ghostly truck that appears out of nowhere, often tailgating them closely. Those who encounter the truck often feel a sense of foreboding, and it mysteriously vanishes when approached, leaving drivers shaken.

3. **Pacific Coast Highway - The Lady in White**: Along the scenic Pacific Coast Highway in California, tales abound of a ghostly figure known as the Lady in White. She is said to appear on the roadside, often trying to flag down passing cars. Legend has it that she died in a car accident while on her way to meet her lover.

4. **Highway 395 - The Ghost of a Fallen Soldier**: In California, along Highway 395, there are stories of a ghostly soldier who appears to motorists, particularly near the area of the Mono Basin. This spirit is believed to be a soldier from the Civil War era, wandering the highway in search of something lost.

5. **US Route 1 - The Ghost of the Old Lighthouse**: Along US Route 1 in Maine, the ghost of a lighthouse keeper is said to haunt the area. Travelers have reported seeing strange lights emanating from the old lighthouse at night, and some claim to hear the echoes of distant bell tolls, believed to be the ghost trying to guide lost ships to safety.

6. **Interstate 95 - The Weeping Woman**: Along I-95, especially in Florida, drivers have reported encounters with a ghostly woman weeping

by the roadside. This figure is often associated with the legend of La Llorona, a woman who lost her children and now roams the highways, searching for them and warning others of the dangers of the road.

7. **Route 29 - The Ghost of the Fisherman**: In Virginia, Route 29 has its own ghost story involving a fisherman who died in a tragic boating accident. Motorists have reported seeing a ghostly figure standing near the water's edge, casting a line into the water, and some claim to hear the sounds of a fishing reel late at night.

8. **Route 50 - The Scarecrow Ghost**: Known as the "Loneliest Road in America," Route 50 in Nevada has its own share of ghost stories. Some travelers have reported seeing a scarecrow by the roadside that seems to move or change positions, giving rise to tales of a restless spirit guarding the barren landscape.

9. **Highway 101 - The Ghostly Child**: Along Highway 101 in California, there are tales of a ghostly child who wanders the roadside, often appearing lost or in distress. Drivers have reported seeing the child standing alone, only to vanish as they approach, leaving them with an unsettling feeling.

10. **I-10 - The Haunted Rest Areas**: Various rest areas along Interstate 10, particularly in Texas, are rumored to be haunted. Truckers and travelers have shared stories of strange noises, flickering lights, and the feeling of being watched while using the facilities.

These ghost stories reflect the rich tapestry of American folklore and the ways in which highways serve as conduits for tales of the supernatural. They add a layer of intrigue to the traveling experience, reminding drivers that the open road holds more than just a path to their destination.

Ghost stories are a fascinating aspect of folklore, and while they vary widely across cultures, several common elements often emerge. Here are some of the most frequently encountered themes and motifs in ghost stories from around the world:

1. **Restless Spirits**: Many ghost stories feature spirits of the deceased who have unfinished business or unresolved issues. This may include seeking closure, avenging a wrong, or delivering a message to the living. The idea of restless spirits is prevalent in cultures that believe in an afterlife or reincarnation.

2. **Tragic Deaths**: Ghosts often arise from tragic or violent deaths. Stories frequently recount events such as murders, accidents, or untimely deaths that leave the spirit tethered to the physical world. This element highlights the emotional weight of loss and the impact of unresolved grief.

3. **Curses and Vengeance**: Many ghost stories involve curses placed on individuals or families, often as a result of wrongdoing. Ghosts may seek vengeance against those who wronged them in life, creating a cycle of retribution that echoes through generations.

4. **Haunted Locations**: Ghosts are commonly associated with specific locations, such as abandoned buildings, graveyards, or historical sites. These places often carry a sense of history, and their eerie atmospheres heighten the fear of the unknown. The idea of haunted locations can serve as a reflection of cultural beliefs about the past.

5. **Warnings and Omens**: Ghosts may appear as harbingers of danger or bad fortune, offering warnings to the living. In some cultures, these apparitions act as protectors, guiding individuals away from harm or alerting them to impending peril.

6. **Symbolism of the Unseen**: Ghost stories often explore themes of the unseen and the unknown. Spirits may represent fears of death, the afterlife, or the consequences of one's actions. They serve as a vehicle for discussing existential questions and the boundaries between life and death.

7. **Family and Ancestral Connections**: Many ghost stories emphasize connections to family and ancestors. Spirits may return to guide, protect, or communicate with their descendants, reflecting cultural values around lineage, heritage, and respect for the dead.

8. **Cultural Beliefs and Rituals**: Ghost stories are often intertwined with cultural beliefs and rituals surrounding death and the afterlife. They may reflect practices such as ancestor worship, funerary rites, and the importance of honoring the deceased.

9. **Fear of the Unknown**: A pervasive theme in ghost stories is the fear of the unknown. The presence of a ghost often evokes anxiety about what lies beyond death and the mysteries of existence. This fear can serve as a cautionary tale, warning against certain behaviors or choices.

10. **Transformation and Redemption**: Some ghost stories feature themes of transformation or redemption, where a spirit seeks forgiveness or healing. These narratives can illustrate the potential for growth and understanding, even in the face of death.

These common elements reflect the universal human experience of grappling with mortality, loss, and the mysteries of existence. Ghost stories serve as a means of exploring cultural beliefs and values while providing a lens through which to understand the complexities of life and death.

Chapter 5: The Highway of Whispers

As Emily continued her journey down Route 66, she felt a renewed sense of purpose. The road ahead seemed to stretch infinitely, each mile a reminder of the adventures yet to come. However, the memory of her encounter with Jake lingered in her mind, a spectral presence that guided her thoughts as she drove deeper into the heart of the American Southwest.

The Desert Town

One afternoon, Emily found herself in a small, dusty town that seemed frozen in time. The faded storefronts and vintage gas stations whispered stories of a bygone era, and she felt drawn to explore. After parking her truck, she strolled along the main street, taking in the sights and sounds of the quaint town.

As she wandered, she stumbled upon an old diner, its neon sign flickering like a beacon. The smell of freshly brewed coffee wafted through the air, inviting her inside. The diner was sparsely populated, with only a few patrons scattered at the counter. She took a seat at a booth, eager to soak in the atmosphere and perhaps strike up a conversation with the locals.

Tales from the Locals

As Emily sipped her coffee, she struck up a conversation with the waitress, a middle-aged woman named Marjorie. With a warm smile and a twinkle in her eye, Marjorie began sharing tales of the town's history. Emily listened intently as Marjorie recounted stories of travelers who had passed through, some with happy endings, others with darker twists.

"It's funny," Marjorie said, her voice dropping to a conspiratorial whisper. "This town has its fair share of ghost stories. You see, long ago, there was a tragic accident on the highway just outside of town. A couple was driving home after visiting relatives when their car went off the road. They say the woman's spirit still roams the highway, searching for her lost love."

Emily felt a chill run down her spine. She remembered Jake's story about the lost couple and the whispers of love that lingered in the air. "What happened to them?" she asked, intrigued.

"They say the man died on impact, but the woman survived for a short while, clinging to life in the hospital. She never stopped calling for him, and when she passed, her spirit was said to have returned to the highway, forever searching for him," Marjorie replied, her voice filled with reverence.

The Journey Continues

As the sun began to set, casting a golden hue over the desert landscape, Emily thanked Marjorie for the stories and stepped outside. The air was cool, and the sky was painted with streaks of orange and purple. She felt compelled to visit the site of the accident, a place that seemed to echo with the pain of lost love.

Following Marjorie's directions, Emily drove a few miles outside of town until she reached a quiet stretch of highway. Pulling over, she stepped out of her truck and took a deep breath, feeling the weight of history pressing down on her. The highway was serene, but there was an underlying tension in the air, as if the past lingered just beneath the surface.

Whispers in the Wind

As she stood by the roadside, Emily closed her eyes and listened. The wind rustled through the sagebrush, carrying with it the faintest whispers. It was as if the spirits of the lost couple were calling out, searching for each other across the divide of life and death.

"Are you there?" Emily whispered into the stillness, her heart racing. "Can you hear me?"

In that moment, she felt a rush of energy surround her, and for a fleeting second, she thought she saw a figure in the distance—a woman dressed in a flowing white dress, standing by the side of the road, looking for something.

"Is it you?" Emily called out, taking a hesitant step forward. But as she got closer, the figure began to fade, disappearing into the twilight. A sense of longing filled the air, and Emily was overcome with emotion, feeling the weight of the woman's sorrow in her own heart.

A Moment of Connection

As the sun dipped below the horizon, Emily felt an overwhelming urge to honor the love that had been lost. She reached into her truck and retrieved a small bouquet of wildflowers she had picked earlier in the day. Kneeling by the roadside, she placed the flowers gently on the ground, whispering a silent prayer for the couple.

"May you find peace," she murmured. "May your love guide you home."

As she stood up, a gentle breeze swept through, rustling the flowers and sending a shiver down her spine. In that moment, she felt a sense of connection, as if the spirits of the couple had acknowledged her gesture. It was a reminder that love transcends time and space, lingering long after the physical forms have faded.

Reflections on the Journey

Returning to her truck, Emily felt a newfound clarity. The journey she was on was not just a physical one; it was also a journey of healing and understanding. The whispers of the highway echoed in her mind, reminding her that every mile traveled held the potential for connection and discovery.

As she drove away from the site, the stars began to twinkle overhead, illuminating the road ahead. The stories of lost loves and restless spirits would forever be etched in her heart, guiding her as she continued her adventure.

With each passing mile, Emily embraced the uncertainty of the road, knowing that the whispers of the past would always be there, reminding her of the love that endures beyond the boundaries of life and death.

Chapter 6: The Midnight Encounter

As Emily continued her journey along Route 66, the landscapes shifted dramatically from the arid desert to lush, rolling hills. Each twist and turn of the highway revealed new wonders, yet the weight of her experiences lingered with her. The stories of lost love and restless spirits had opened her heart to the mysteries of the road, and she found herself more attuned to the world around her.

An Unexpected Detour

One evening, as the sun dipped below the horizon, casting a warm glow over the hills, Emily decided to take a detour off the main highway. A small sign caught her attention, pointing toward a scenic overlook that promised breathtaking views of the valley below. Intrigued, she turned off the road and followed the winding path that led to the overlook.

As she parked her truck and stepped out, Emily was greeted by a stunning vista. The valley spread out before her, bathed in the soft light of twilight. She took a deep breath, feeling a sense of peace wash over her. This was why she had embarked on this journey—to experience the beauty of the world and to find herself along the way.

The Sound of Laughter

As she stood at the edge of the overlook, lost in thought, she suddenly heard laughter drifting through the air. It was light and carefree, echoing through the trees. Curiosity piqued, Emily followed the sound, moving cautiously down a narrow path that led into the woods.

The laughter grew louder, and soon she found herself in a small clearing illuminated by the silvery light of the moon. To her surprise, she discovered a group of people gathered around a flickering campfire, their faces lit with joy and camaraderie. They were a mix of ages—friends, families, and couples—sharing stories and laughter beneath the starlit sky.

Emily hesitated at the edge of the clearing, unsure if she should approach. But before she could turn back, one of the women in the group spotted her and waved her over.

"Hey there! Come join us!" she called, her smile infectious. "We could use another storyteller around the fire!"

A Warm Welcome

Feeling drawn to the warmth of the gathering, Emily stepped forward. As she joined the circle, the group welcomed her with open arms, offering her food and a seat by the fire. They shared stories of their own travels, recounting adventures and misadventures with laughter and nostalgia.

As the night wore on, Emily felt a sense of belonging among these strangers. They shared tales of ghost sightings and local legends, recounting their own encounters with spirits along various highways. One man spoke of a haunted bridge where a couple had met their tragic end, while another shared a story of a ghostly figure that appeared to warn drivers of impending danger.

The Ghostly Tale

As the fire crackled and the stars twinkled overhead, Emily felt inspired to share her own story. She recounted her encounter with the lost couple's spirit and the whispers she had heard on the highway. The group listened intently, captivated by her tale.

"Love is a powerful thing," one woman remarked, her eyes glistening with emotion. "It transcends everything, even death. Those spirits are still connected to this world because of their love."

As the conversation flowed, Emily felt a profound connection to the group. They were all travelers, each with their own stories and experiences, bound together by the shared journey of life.

A Haunting Presence

Just as the night began to wind down, a sudden chill swept through the clearing. The laughter faded, replaced by an eerie stillness. Emily felt a tingling sensation on the back of her neck, as if she were being watched. The group fell silent, exchanging uneasy glances.

"What was that?" one of the men whispered, his voice barely audible.

Before anyone could respond, a soft whisper echoed through the trees, barely discernible above the rustling leaves. It was a haunting melody, a lullaby that seemed to drift on the wind. The group looked around nervously, uncertainty hanging in the air.

"I think it's the spirits," the woman who had welcomed Emily said softly. "They're here with us."

Embracing the Unknown

Despite the unease, Emily felt a strange sense of comfort. She closed her eyes and focused on the whispering melody, allowing it to wash over her. In that moment, she realized that the presence of the spirits was a reminder of the love and connections that transcended time.

"Maybe they're here to remind us of the importance of love," Emily said, her voice steady. "To cherish the moments we have with each other."

The group nodded in agreement, finding solace in her words. The whispers continued, and for a moment, it felt as if the spirits were weaving their stories into the fabric of the night.

A Night to Remember

As the fire began to die down, the group decided to share one last story—a tale of hope and resilience. They took turns sharing memories of loved ones lost and the lessons learned from their journeys. The atmosphere shifted from fear to gratitude, embracing the idea that even in loss, there is beauty.

When the night finally came to an end, the group exchanged contact information, promising to stay in touch as they embarked on their separate paths. Emily felt a sense of gratitude for the unexpected encounter, knowing that she had connected with kindred spirits along her journey.

As she walked back to her truck, she glanced back at the clearing one last time. The campfire had burned low, but the memories of the night would linger in her heart. The whispers of the past, the laughter of new friends, and the stories shared would guide her as she continued along the winding road of life.

With a renewed sense of purpose, Emily climbed into her truck and set off into the night, ready to embrace whatever adventures awaited her on the highway of whispers.

Chapter 7: The Keeper of Secrets

As the sun rose on a new day, painting the sky in soft pastels, Emily felt invigorated by her experiences from the night before. The warmth of the campfire and the laughter of newfound friends lingered in her heart, reminding her of the beauty of connections formed along the journey. With renewed energy, she set out once more on Route 66, eager to see where the road would lead her next.

The Town of Mysteries

Emily drove for several hours, the landscape shifting from rolling hills to vast plains dotted with wildflowers. Eventually, she stumbled upon a small town that seemed to call out to her. Its name, "Mystic Hollow," was painted in faded letters above the entrance. Intrigued, she pulled over, feeling an inexplicable pull to explore its secrets.

The town was quaint, with charming shops lining the main street and a sense of history in the air. As she wandered, she discovered a small bookstore with an inviting window display. The sign above the door read "The Keeper of Secrets." Drawn to it, Emily stepped inside, the scent of old books and fresh coffee enveloping her.

An Unexpected Encounter

Inside the bookstore, the atmosphere was cozy and intimate. Shelves were lined with books of every genre, some with worn spines that hinted at their age. At the back of the store sat an elderly woman, her silver hair pulled back in a neat bun, surrounded by stacks of books. She looked up as Emily entered, her eyes twinkling with wisdom.

"Welcome, dear traveler," the woman said, her voice warm and inviting. "I see you've come seeking stories."

Emily smiled, feeling an instant connection. "I love stories, especially those that carry the whispers of the past."

The woman nodded knowingly. "Ah, but every story comes with its secrets. Some are meant to be shared, while others are best left untold. What brings you to Mystic Hollow?"

The Tale of the Forgotten

As Emily shared her journey and the tales she had encountered, the woman listened intently, her gaze never wavering. After Emily finished, the woman leaned forward, her voice lowering to a conspiratorial tone.

"There is a story hidden in this town, one that has been forgotten by many but still lingers in the shadows. It's about a young woman who vanished many years ago, leaving behind a trail of questions and a heartbroken lover."

Emily leaned closer, her curiosity piqued. "What happened to her?"

"It is said that she and her lover were deeply in love but faced opposition from their families. On the night they planned to elope, she disappeared without a trace. Many believe her spirit still roams the area, searching for her lost love."

The Keeper of Secrets

Intrigued, Emily asked, "Do you think her spirit is still here? Can you feel her presence?"

The woman smiled softly, her eyes reflecting a depth of understanding. "The past has a way of lingering, even when we try to forget. Some spirits remain tied to the earth, seeking closure or resolution. The whispers of their stories can be felt by those who are willing to listen."

As she spoke, a shiver ran down Emily's spine. The connection between love and loss resonated deeply within her, echoing her own experiences along the road.

"Would you like to know more about her story?" the woman asked, her tone inviting.

Emily nodded eagerly, feeling a sense of destiny in the air. "Yes, please."

A Journey into the Past

The woman led Emily to a dusty corner of the bookstore, where a collection of old journals and newspapers lay scattered. She carefully picked up a leather-bound journal and began to read aloud excerpts that told of the young couple's love, their dreams, and the night of the fateful elopement.

As the story unfolded, Emily felt a connection building—not just to the woman from the past, but to the universal experience of love and heartbreak. The journal revealed the couple's hopes, fears, and the turmoil they faced, painting a vivid picture of their lives.

"The young woman's name was Clara," the woman said softly. "She was known for her kindness and spirit. The night she vanished, her lover searched for her, but it was as if she had simply vanished into thin air."

The Unraveling of Secrets

As the woman continued reading, Emily felt a sense of urgency growing within her. "What happened to her lover? Did he ever find her?"

The woman closed the journal, her expression somber. "He spent his life searching for her, never giving up hope. Some say he still wanders these woods, listening for her voice, hoping to reunite with her one day. Others believe that Clara's spirit roams in search of him, forever bound to the place where their love was meant to flourish."

Emily's heart ached at the thought of their undying love. "Is there a way to help them find peace?"

The woman nodded slowly. "Sometimes, the living can bridge the gap between the worlds. If you're willing, you could go to the place where she last disappeared and honor their love. It may help both spirits find closure."

The Call to Action

Feeling a sense of purpose, Emily took a deep breath. "I want to help. Where do I need to go?"

The woman handed her a small map, marking the location of a secluded glade deep within the woods, near the edge of town. "Follow this path, and you may find what you seek. Remember, love has a way of transcending even the darkest shadows."

With gratitude, Emily thanked the woman and prepared to embark on her new quest. As she stepped outside, the sun was beginning to set, casting a golden light over Mystic Hollow. She felt a sense of determination and connection to the past, ready to honor the love that had endured through the ages.

The Path Ahead

As Emily ventured into the woods, the sounds of nature surrounded her—the rustling leaves, the chirping of crickets, and the gentle whisper of the wind. She followed the path, feeling the weight of history on her shoulders. The deeper she went, the more she felt the presence of Clara's spirit guiding her.

Eventually, she arrived at a small clearing, the air thick with emotion. Emily knelt down, gathered a handful of wildflowers, and arranged them in a circle on the ground—an offering to the spirits of Clara and her lover.

"May you find peace," she whispered, her voice carried by the wind. "May your love guide you home."

As she sat in silence, listening to the whispers of the past, Emily felt a sense of fulfillment wash over her. The journey had led her to this moment, and she knew that love, whether lost or found, would always be a guiding light along the winding road.

Chapter 8: The Glade of Echoes

The sun dipped below the horizon, casting an ethereal glow over the glade where Emily knelt, surrounded by the wildflowers she had gathered. The air was thick with the scent of earth and blossoms, and the stillness of the moment enveloped her like a warm embrace. It was here, in this sacred space, that she hoped to connect with the spirits of Clara and her lost love.

A Whisper from the Past

As Emily sat quietly, she closed her eyes and focused on the rhythmic sounds of nature—the rustling leaves, the distant call of a bird, and the gentle rustle of the wind through the trees. She felt a shift in the atmosphere, as if the very air around her was charged with emotion. It was then that she heard it: a soft whisper, barely audible, weaving through the leaves.

"Clara... where are you?"

The voice was faint but filled with longing, echoing through the glade like a haunting melody. Emily's heart raced as she opened her eyes, feeling the presence of something otherworldly surrounding her. It was as if Clara's spirit had responded to her offering, calling out in search of her lost love.

"Clara?" Emily whispered into the stillness, her voice trembling with anticipation. "I'm here to honor your love and help you find peace."

The Vision of Love

Suddenly, a shimmering light flickered in the clearing, and Emily felt a rush of energy enveloping her. She blinked, and before her eyes, the figure of a young woman appeared, ethereal and radiant. Clara stood before her, her flowing dress glimmering like moonlight, her expression a mix of sorrow and hope.

"Thank you for coming," Clara's voice echoed softly, like a gentle breeze. "I have waited so long for someone to hear my call."

Emily felt tears welling up in her eyes. "I'm here to help you. I heard your story, and I want to reunite you with your love. Can you tell me what happened that night?"

A Tale of Heartbreak

Clara's gaze turned distant, and she seemed lost in a memory. "We had planned to elope, to escape the confines of our families' expectations. But on that fateful night, I was frightened and ran into the woods to gather my thoughts. I lost my way, and in my panic, I stumbled and fell. When I awoke, I was alone... and he was searching for me."

Emily's heart ached for the young woman before her. "You've been searching for him ever since, haven't you?"

Clara nodded, her eyes glistening with unshed tears. "I can feel his presence, but he cannot see me. I am trapped between worlds, a whisper of what once was."

The Search for Closure

"Clara," Emily said gently, "your love is still with you. He has never forgotten you. If you can guide me to where you last saw him, perhaps I can help you find closure."

Clara's expression shifted, a glimmer of hope igniting in her eyes. "There is a place near the old bridge where he called my name, where our hearts were intertwined. If you can take me there, I believe we can finally find peace."

Emily rose to her feet, determination coursing through her veins. "Lead the way."

The Journey to the Bridge

Clara's spirit floated gracefully ahead of Emily, guiding her through the woods. As they walked, the atmosphere shifted, the air growing cooler and filled with an electric energy. It felt as though they were moving through a tapestry of memories, each step resonating with the echoes of love and longing.

After what felt like an eternity, they arrived at the old bridge. It spanned a gentle stream, the water glistening under the moonlight, and the wooden beams creaked softly in the silence. Emily could feel the weight of history in the air, as if the bridge had witnessed countless stories of love and loss.

Clara paused at the edge of the bridge, her translucent form shimmering in the moonlight. "This is where he called for me," she whispered. "This is where our hearts were meant to unite."

A Heartfelt Reunion

As Emily stood beside Clara, she closed her eyes and concentrated, envisioning the young man who had loved Clara so deeply. "I call upon you," she spoke softly, her voice steady. "If you are here, please hear my words. Clara is searching for you. She has waited for so long."

The wind picked up, swirling around them like a gentle caress. Emily felt a sudden rush of energy, and in that moment, she sensed another presence joining them. A figure began to materialize on the other side of the bridge—a young man, looking just as Clara had described. His expression was one of confusion mixed with hope, and as he took a step forward, Emily's heart raced.

"Clara?" he called out, his voice filled with longing. "Is that you?"

Clara's spirit glowed brighter, her joy palpable. "I'm here, my love! I have come back to you."

The Moment of Connection

The two spirits stood on either side of the bridge, a shimmering connection forming between them. Emily watched in awe as their energies intertwined, creating a radiant light that illuminated the night. It was a moment of pure love, transcending the boundaries of life and death.

"Forever," the young man whispered, his eyes filled with tears. "I never stopped searching for you."

"I never stopped waiting," Clara replied, her voice a soft melody. "Now we can finally be together."

As their spirits embraced, a wave of warmth washed over Emily, filling her with a sense of peace and fulfillment. The love that had once been lost was now reunited, and the weight of their sorrow began to lift.

A Whisper of Freedom

In that moment, Emily understood the power of love and the importance of honoring the past. Clara and her lover had finally found closure, their spirits free to move on together. As their forms began to fade, they turned to Emily, gratitude shining in their eyes.

"Thank you," Clara's voice echoed softly. "You have given us the gift of freedom."

As the last traces of their spirits vanished into the night, Emily felt a sense of lightness in her heart. The glade, once heavy with sorrow, now felt alive with the echoes of love and hope.

The Road Ahead

Feeling renewed, Emily stood at the edge of the bridge, the moonlight guiding her path. She knew that her journey was far from over, but she carried with her the lessons learned from Clara and her lost love. The whispers of the past would continue to guide her, reminding her of the power of connection and the importance of cherishing every moment.

As she walked back to her truck, the stars twinkled overhead, each one a reminder of the stories woven into the fabric of the universe. With a heart full of hope, Emily set off once again on Route 66, ready to embrace whatever adventures awaited her on the horizon.

Chapter 9: The Road of Reflections

As dawn broke over Mystic Hollow, Emily felt a profound sense of peace settle within her. The reunion of Clara and her lost love had been a powerful reminder of the enduring nature of love, transcending even the boundaries of life and death. With each mile she drove along Route 66, she carried their story in her heart, a beacon guiding her through the twists and turns ahead.

A New Perspective

Continuing her journey, Emily found herself reflecting on the stories she had encountered and the connections she had forged. The road had become more than just a means of travel; it was a tapestry woven with the fabric of human experience—each thread representing love, loss, and the enduring quest for meaning.

As she drove, the landscape began to change once again, with the vast desert giving way to lush valleys and towering mountains. She felt invigorated by the scenery, the beauty of nature resonating with her soul. It was as if the world around her was alive, echoing the stories of those who had traveled this path before her.

The Roadside Attraction

After a few hours, Emily spotted a quirky roadside attraction—a giant, brightly painted dinosaur looming over a small gift shop. Intrigued, she pulled over to explore. As she stepped inside, the shop was filled with an eclectic mix of souvenirs, local crafts, and kitschy memorabilia.

The shopkeeper, an older man with a twinkle in his eye, greeted her warmly. "Welcome! You've stumbled upon the happiest dinosaur in America! What brings you this way?"

"I'm just traveling along Route 66," Emily replied, a smile spreading across her face. "Looking for stories and adventures."

"Well, you've come to the right place! This highway is full of tales—some funny, some spooky. You wouldn't believe the things people have seen along these roads," he said, leaning on the counter.

Sharing Stories

Emily felt an instant connection with the shopkeeper. "I've heard quite a few stories myself. Just last night, I helped a spirit find closure with her lost love."

The man's eyes widened, and he leaned in closer. "Now that's a tale worth telling! You should share it with the customers. People love a good ghost story around here."

With his encouragement, Emily shared her experience with Clara and the reunion at the glade. The shopkeeper listened intently, nodding as she spoke, and soon other customers gathered around to hear her story. Laughter and gasps of surprise filled the shop as she recounted the details, and she felt a sense of joy in sharing the connection she had made with the spirits.

A Generous Gift

After her story concluded, the shopkeeper beamed with appreciation. "You've brightened our day with that one! Here, take this as a token of gratitude." He handed her a small, intricately carved wooden dinosaur. "It's a good luck charm for your travels. May it remind you of the magic of the road and the stories that connect us all."

Emily accepted the gift with gratitude, touched by his kindness. "Thank you! I'll cherish it."

As she prepared to leave, a young girl approached her, clutching a small notebook. "Can I write down your story?" she asked, her eyes wide with curiosity. "I want to remember it!"

"Of course!" Emily replied, feeling honored. The girl eagerly took notes as Emily shared more of her journey, her heart swelling with the joy of storytelling.

The Spirit of Adventure

After saying her goodbyes and thanking the shopkeeper once more, Emily climbed back into her truck, the wooden dinosaur resting on the dashboard. She felt invigorated, her spirit lifted by the connections she had made that day. The road seemed to call to her, urging her to continue her adventure.

As she drove further along Route 66, she pondered the stories of the people she had met—the waitress in the diner, the travelers around the campfire, and now the kind shopkeeper and the inquisitive girl. Each encounter enriched her journey, weaving a tapestry of shared experiences that transcended the miles traveled.

A Moment of Reflection

Stopping at a scenic overlook, Emily stepped out of her truck and took a moment to absorb the view. The valley stretched out before her, bathed in sunlight, and she felt a deep sense of gratitude for the journey she was on. It was not just about the destination but about the connections made along the way.

With the wooden dinosaur in hand, she reflected on the importance of love and storytelling. Each story held the power to heal, to connect, and to remind people of the beauty in vulnerability. She thought of Clara and her lover, their love now set free, and felt a renewed sense of purpose in her own life.

Embracing the Future

As Emily continued her drive, she felt a shift within herself. The experiences she had gathered along the way had transformed her, and she was ready to embrace whatever lay ahead. The road was still long, but she knew that each bend would bring new stories, new encounters, and new opportunities for connection.

With a heart full of hope and a spirit ready for adventure, Emily pressed onward, determined to honor the stories of the past while creating her own narrative on the highway of life. The journey was far from over, and she was excited to see where it would take her next.

Chapter 10: The Crossing of Paths

As Emily continued her journey along Route 66, the sun began to dip low in the sky, casting long shadows across the highway. The warmth of the day lingered, but a cool breeze hinted at the approaching evening. With the wooden dinosaur resting on her dashboard, she felt a sense of adventure bubbling within her. The stories she had collected were weaving together, creating a rich tapestry that filled her heart with purpose.

An Unexpected Encounter

As she drove, Emily noticed a hitchhiker standing at the side of the road, thumb outstretched. He was a young man with tousled hair and a worn backpack, looking as if he had seen his fair share of the open road. After a brief moment of hesitation, she pulled over.

"Need a ride?" she called out, rolling down the window.

The young man smiled gratefully and opened the passenger door. "Thanks! I'm Mark. I've been traveling for a while now, trying to find my way."

"Emily," she replied, extending her hand. "Where are you headed?"

"I'm not really sure," Mark admitted as he settled into the seat. "Just wherever the road takes me. I'm looking for something... maybe a bit of adventure, or perhaps I'm trying to escape something."

A Shared Journey

As they drove, Mark shared his story. He had been traveling across the country after a tough breakup, seeking clarity and healing on the open road. Emily listened intently, finding solace in his words. They talked about their experiences, the freedom of the road, and the weight of emotional burdens that sometimes felt too heavy to carry alone.

"I think the road has a way of teaching us what we need to learn," Emily mused, glancing at the passing scenery. "Every encounter, every story—it all shapes who we are."

Mark nodded. "Yeah, I feel that. It's like each mile brings a new perspective. I've met some incredible people along the way, and it's helped me see things differently."

The Spirit of Adventure

As they continued down Route 66, Emily felt a connection growing between them. Mark's easygoing nature and openness resonated with her own journey, and she found herself sharing her own stories—the encounters with Clara, the campfire tales, and the kindness of the shopkeeper.

"Wow, it sounds like you've had some amazing experiences," Mark said, his eyes wide with interest. "I've always believed that stories have power. They can heal, inspire, and even connect people in ways we can't always understand."

Emily smiled, appreciating his insight. "Exactly! Each story is a thread that binds us together, reminding us that we're not alone in our struggles."

The Ghost Town

As dusk began to settle, they approached an old ghost town, its abandoned buildings silhouetted against the fading light. Curious, Emily pulled off the highway to explore. The town, once bustling with life, now stood eerily quiet, filled with remnants of the past.

"Let's check it out," Mark suggested, his eyes sparkling with excitement.

They stepped out of the truck and wandered through the dusty streets, taking in the crumbling facades and rusted signs. A sense of nostalgia hung in the air, as if the spirits of those who once lived there still lingered.

Echoes of the Past

As they walked, they stumbled upon an old saloon, its door hanging ajar. Emily hesitated for a moment but then pushed the door open, revealing a dimly lit interior. The wooden floors creaked beneath their feet, and the scent of aged whiskey and dust filled the air.

"Wow, this place is something else," Mark said, glancing around. "Can you imagine the stories that must have been shared here?"

Emily nodded, her imagination running wild. "I can almost hear the laughter and the music. It's like stepping back in time."

As they explored the saloon, Emily felt a chill run down her spine. The atmosphere was thick with history, and she sensed the echoes of the past whispering through the air. It was as if the spirits of the town were inviting them to listen to their stories.

A Haunting Presence

Suddenly, a soft breeze swept through the saloon, sending a shiver through Emily. She glanced at Mark, who had gone quiet, his eyes fixed on a corner of the room. Following his gaze, she saw a faint shimmer—an ethereal figure standing by the bar.

"Do you see that?" she whispered, her heart racing.

Mark nodded slowly, his expression a mix of awe and disbelief. "What is it?"

The figure began to take shape, revealing the outline of a woman in a vintage dress, her expression a blend of sadness and longing. Emily felt an overwhelming urge to connect with her spirit, to understand her story.

A Connection Across Time

"Hello?" Emily called out, her voice steady yet gentle. "Can you hear us?"

The figure turned, her gaze locking onto Emily. "I am Rose," she whispered, her voice barely audible. "I once lived here, in this town. I loved and lost, and my spirit remains bound to this place."

Mark and Emily exchanged glances, both captivated by the revelation. "What happened to you, Rose?" Emily asked, her heart aching for the spirit.

"I waited for him," Rose replied, her voice a haunting melody. "He never returned. I lost hope and became a shadow of my former self, forever searching for what was lost."

A Chance for Closure

Emily's heart swelled with compassion. "You don't have to remain trapped here. Your love deserves to be honored, and you can find peace."

Rose's gaze softened, and Emily felt a connection between them—a shared understanding of love's power. "Will you help me?" Rose asked, her voice trembling. "Help me find closure so that I may finally move on."

Mark stepped forward, his expression resolute. "We'll help you, Rose. Just tell us what we need to do."

The Ritual of Remembrance

Rose's ethereal form glowed brighter as she spoke. "Take me to the old oak tree by the river, where we used to meet. There, we can honor our love and release the bonds that tie me to this world."

With determination, Emily and Mark led Rose's spirit out of the saloon and toward the riverbank, the fading light of day casting an otherworldly glow on their path. They reached the ancient oak tree, its gnarled branches reaching toward the sky.

"Gather some flowers," Rose instructed. "We will create a circle of remembrance."

As they collected wildflowers, Emily felt a sense of purpose. Together, they arranged the blossoms in a circle beneath the oak tree, creating a sacred space for Rose's spirit.

The Final Goodbye

As they knelt in reverence, Emily closed her eyes and spoke softly. "Rose, we honor your love and the memories you hold dear. May you find peace as you release the past."

Mark joined in, his voice strong. "Your love story deserves to be celebrated. Let go of the pain, and embrace the freedom that awaits you."

As they spoke, a warm breeze swept through the clearing, and Rose's spirit began to shimmer. "Thank you," she whispered, her voice filled with gratitude. "I can feel the weight lifting. I am ready to be free."

At that moment, the bond between Rose and her lost love began to glow, illuminating the night. As the final remnants of her spirit coalesced, she whispered, "Forever in love, forever in peace."

With a final shimmer, Rose's spirit ascended into the night sky, leaving behind a sense of tranquility that enveloped Emily and Mark. They sat in silence, absorbing the beauty of the moment, feeling the echoes of love and loss intertwining in the air.

A New Understanding

As they made their way back to the truck, Emily and Mark exchanged knowing smiles. The experience deepened their connection, and they understood the importance of honoring the past while embracing the future.

"Thank you for sharing this with me," Mark said, his voice sincere. "I didn't expect to encounter something so profound today."

Emily smiled back, feeling a sense of fulfillment. "It's moments like these that remind us of the magic we can find on the road. Every story matters, and every spirit deserves to be heard."

As they drove away from the ghost town, the stars twinkled overhead, illuminating the path ahead. Emily felt a renewed sense of purpose in her journey, knowing that the road would continue to lead her to new stories, new encounters, and new opportunities to connect.

With Mark by her side, she was ready to embrace whatever lay ahead, knowing that together they could navigate the highways of life, carrying the echoes of the past while forging their own stories along the way.

Conclusion: The Road Continues

As Emily and Mark continued their journey along Route 66, the open road stretched out before them like a canvas waiting to be painted with new memories. The encounters they had shared—the stories of lost loves, restless spirits, and the connections forged through shared experiences—had transformed them both. Each mile traveled was a testament to the resilience of the human spirit and the enduring power of love.

A Journey of Healing

Through Clara and her lover, Rose, and the many others they encountered along the way, Emily had come to understand that every story holds a piece of truth, a reflection of the complexities of life. The road had become a metaphor for her own journey—a path of healing, discovery, and connection.

With Mark by her side, she felt a renewed sense of purpose. They had both come to the road seeking something—adventure, clarity, healing—and together they had found it in the stories shared, the spirits honored, and the love that transcended the boundaries of life and death.

Embracing New Beginnings

As they drove under a sky filled with stars, Emily felt a sense of freedom she had never known before. The weight of her past had begun to lift, replaced by a sense of hope and possibility. The wooden dinosaur, a token of luck and magic, sat proudly on her dashboard, a reminder of the kindness she had encountered and the stories that had shaped her journey.

"I never imagined this trip would lead me to so many incredible experiences," she said to Mark, glancing over at him. "It's like every stop has revealed something new about myself."

Mark nodded a smile on his face. "It's amazing what happens when we open ourselves up to the journey. The road has a way of teaching us what we need to learn."

The Spirit of Adventure

With each passing town and each shared story, Emily felt more connected to the world around her. She realized that the journey was not just about reaching a destination; it was about the moments shared with others, the connections made, and the love that flows through every experience.

As they continued down the highway, Emily and Mark spoke of their dreams for the future—of new adventures, new stories to tell, and the possibility of forging a deeper connection. The road ahead was uncertain, but they were ready to embrace it together, knowing that whatever lay ahead would be woven into the fabric of their shared narrative.

A Tapestry of Stories

Emily understood that the stories she had collected were more than just tales of the past; they were threads that connected her to the present and the future. Each encounter enriched her understanding of love, loss, and the beauty of human connection. She felt a profound sense of gratitude for the journey that had led her to this moment.

As the night deepened and the stars twinkled overhead, Emily knew that the road would continue to unfold before her, filled with endless possibilities. With a heart full of hope and a spirit eager for adventure, she was ready to embrace whatever came next.

The highway of life is long and winding, filled with stories waiting to be discovered. And as Emily and Mark drove on, they carried with them the echoes of those stories—a reminder that love knows no bounds and that every journey, no matter how far, is enriched by the connections we make along the way.

And so, with the wind in their hair and the open road ahead, they ventured forth, ready to write the next chapter of their lives, one mile at a time.

Source Material

1. **Literature on Travel and Adventure:**

- *On the Road* by Jack Kerouac: A classic novel that captures the spirit of adventure and the quest for meaning along America's highways.

- *Blue Highways* by William Least Heat-Moon: A travel memoir exploring backroads and the stories of people who met along the way.

2. **Ghost Stories and Folklore:**

- *Ghosts of America* by various authors: A collection of ghost stories and legends from across the United States, highlighting the connection between love and loss.

- Local folklore and urban legends pertaining to Route 66: Stories of hauntings, lost loves, and the spirits of travelers who once roamed the highway.

3. **Themes of Love and Loss:**

- *The Fault in Our Stars* by John Green: A poignant exploration of love and loss that resonates with the experiences of young couples facing tragic circumstances.

- *A Walk to Remember* by Nicholas Sparks: A love story that delves into themes of enduring love and the impact of loss.

4. **Travel Guides and Historical Accounts:**

- *Route 66: The Mother Road* by Michael Wallis: A comprehensive history of the iconic highway, detailing its significance in American culture and travel.

- *The Great American Road Trip* by various authors: Guides that explore the cultural and historical significance of various routes across the United States.

5. **Spirituality and Self-Discovery:**

- *Eat, Pray, Love* by Elizabeth Gilbert: A memoir about self-discovery through travel, exploring themes of love, healing, and personal growth.

- *The Alchemist* by Paulo Coelho: A philosophical novel about pursuing one's dreams and the journey of self-discovery.

6. **Nature and Reflection:**

- *Wild* by Cheryl Strayed: A memoir about personal healing through a journey on the Pacific Crest Trail, emphasizing the connection between nature and self-discovery.

- Nature writing from authors like John Muir and Henry David Thoreau, who emphasize the importance of the natural world in personal reflection and growth.

7. **Cultural Studies:**

- Studies on the significance of storytelling in different cultures, examining how narratives shape identity and community.

- Research on the psychological impact of travel and exploration on personal development and healing.

Additional Inspirations

- **Personal Travel Experiences:** Insights and anecdotes from travelers who have taken journeys along Route 66 or other iconic American roads.

- **Art and Media:** Films and documentaries that explore themes of travel, adventure, and the human experience, such as *The Motorcycle Diaries* or *Into the Wild*.

- **Music:** Songs that evoke themes of longing, love, and the open road, which can serve as a backdrop to the emotions conveyed in the narrative.

As a 29-year- veteran truck driver, I've always been captivated by the stories that unfold on the open road. Each mile I travel is an opportunity to witness the rich tapestry of life that exists beyond the confines of my cab. The adventures of Emily along Route 66 resonate with me deeply, as they encapsulate the essence of what it means to journey through life—filled with encounters, reflections, and the search for connection.

The tales of love, loss, and healing that Emily experiences remind me of the countless stories I've encountered during my own travels. From quiet towns to bustling cities, every stop has its own narrative, waiting to be discovered. These stories have a way of weaving themselves into our lives, shaping our perspectives, and enriching our understanding of the world around us.

As I navigate the highways, I often think of the people I meet—fellow truck drivers, locals, and travelers—each carrying their own unique experiences. The road has taught me that we are all interconnected, bound by our shared humanity. Just like Emily, I find joy in listening to these stories, knowing that they hold the power to inspire, heal, and connect us in ways we may not fully comprehend.

In sharing this journey through the pages of this book, I hope to convey the magic of the open road and the importance of embracing the experiences that come our way. Life, much like a long-haul truck ride, is filled with unexpected turns and opportunities for growth. It's a reminder to cherish the moments, honor the past, and remain open to the possibilities that lie ahead.

Thank you for joining me on this journey. May you find your own stories along the road, and may they inspire you to seek out new adventures, forge meaningful connections, and embrace the beautiful complexity of life. Safe travels, and may the road always lead you to new horizons!

Keep on Trucking!!

Don't miss out!

Visit the website below and you can sign up to receive emails whenever Joseph Capps publishes a new book. There's no charge and no obligation.

https://books2read.com/r/B-A-YHBMC-QWFAF

BOOKS 2 READ

Connecting independent readers to independent writers.

Also by Joseph Capps

ChatGPT for Beginners: A Comprehensive Guide
Whispers from Beyond: An Exploration of Ghosts and the Paranormal"
Haunting Highways: Real-Life Ghost Stories from Truck Drivers
The Road Ahead: A Comprehensive Guide to Trucking in the United States

About the Author

Joseph Capps is a new author passionate about weaving stories that inspire and entertain. With a background in [your field or interests], he brings a fresh perspective to his writing, blending imagination with relatable themes. Joseph's debut work reflects his love for [the unknown and paranormal], inviting readers into worlds filled with rich characters and compelling narratives.

When he's not writing, Joseph enjoys [riding his motorcycle], drawing inspiration from everyday experiences. He currently resides in [East Tennessee], where he is excited to continue his journey as a storyteller.

Feel free to customize any part of this bio to better reflect your personality and writing style!

About the Publisher

I am 49-year-old retired truck driver. From North East Tennessee. I started writing books for something to fill my time. I have enjoyed the experience So far.

www.ingramcontent.com/pod-product-compliance
Lightning Source LLC
Chambersburg PA
CBHW021809150726
47989CB00004B/1854